To:

From:

Copyright © 2012 Hallmark Licensing, Inc.

Published by Hallmark Gift Books,
a division of Hallmark Cards, Inc.,
Kansas City, MO 64141
Visit us on the Web at www.Hallmark.com.

Editor: Chelsea Fogleman
Art Director: Kevin Swanson
Illustrator: Scott Brown
Production Artist: Dan Horton

ISBN: 978-1-59530-463-6
EWM3029

Printed and bound in China
NOV11

The Egg-cellent Mama Hen

Hallmark
GIFT BOOKS

by **Bill Gray** Illustrated by **Scott Brown**

Mama Henrietta was an egg-ceptional little hen
who didn't lay eggs just every now and then . . .

She laid eggs in the morning. She laid them late at night.
She even laid eggs in her sleep. (Yeah, you heard me right!)

And here's a little secret: Those eggs that she would lay . . .
She didn't just lay them. She gave them all away!
She never hesitated. She never thought twice.
Those eggs were extra festive, and she was extra nice.

Just about the time the rooster finished crowing,
that's when Mama Henrietta started to get going.
She strutted down the road. She waddled into town . . .

. . . and every seven steps or so,
an egg rolled on the ground.

There were many friends to visit, lots of things to do,
and every place that Mama stopped, she left an egg or two.

She said, "Good day, sir!" at the bridge and left one for the toll.
She popped into a donut shop and left one in a hole.

She had a mochaccino with biscotti she could dip.
She paid the waitress with an egg (and left one for the tip!).

At Mrs. Cluck's Hat Shoppe, she picked out a new bonnet.
But it didn't look quite right until she laid an egg upon it.

Down at Daisy Park where the animals run loose,
she met Billy Bull and his good friend Suzy Goose.
Suzy got some polka dots, and zig zags went to Billy.
Mama's eggs were beautiful . . . and sometimes kinda silly!

Just about the hour when the sun slid down the sky,
Mama Henrietta knew the time had come to fly.
Except, of course, she couldn't fly. (Chickens can't, you know!)
So she squawked for a taxi and told it where to go.

When she got back home, all her chicks gathered round
to hear the adventures of Mama's day downtown.
She told about the who, the when, the what, the where . . .
the kind of fun you always have when your friends are there!

Later on that night, as her chicks went to bed,
once their beaks were all brushed and their stories all read,
she reminded each one, as they closed their sleepy eyes,
"If you have something good, never keep it inside."

She left a little glowing egg so they would have some light.
Then she gave each chick a kiss and whispered, "Nighty-night."

Did Mama Henrietta's story make you smile?
Give us a squawk!

Please send your comments to:
Hallmark Book Feedback
P.O. Box 419034
Mail Drop 215
Kansas City, MO 64141

Or e-mail us at:
booknotes@hallmark.com